To the teachers and librarians shaping young minds. —H. K.

To all the truth seekers of our time, in hope of a better future. —M. A.

Library of Congress Cataloging-in-Publication Data:
Names: Khan, Hena, author. | Amini, Mehrdokht, illustrator.
Title: Crescent moons and pointed minarets : a Muslim book of shapes / by Hena Khan ; illustrated by Mehrdokht Amini.
Description: San Francisco, California : Chronicle Books LLC, [2018] |
Summary: In simple rhyming text a young Muslim girl guides the reader through the traditions and shapes of Islam.
Identifiers: LCCN 2017007553| ISBN 9781452155418 (alk. paper) | ISBN 1452155410 (alk. paper)
Subjects: LCSH: Islam—Customs and practices—Juvenile fiction. | Muslims—Juvenile fiction. | Shapes—Juvenile fiction. | CYAC: Stories
in rhyme. | Islam—Customs and practices—Fiction. | Muslims—Fiction. | Shape—Fiction. | LCGFT: Stories in rhyme.
Classification: LCC PZ8.3.K493 Cr 2018 | DDC [E]—dc23 LC record available at https://lccn.loc.gov/2017007553

Manufactured in China.

Design by Amelia Mack.
Typeset in Tournedot.
The illustrations in this book were rendered in mixed media.

10 9 8 7 6 5 4 3

Chronicle Books LLC
680 Second Street
San Francisco, California 94107

Chronicle Books—we see things differently. Become part of our community at www.chroniclekids.com.

Crescent Moons and Pointed Minarets

A Muslim Book of Shapes

by Hena Khan

illustrated by

Mehrdokht Amini

chronicle books · san francisco

Cone is the tip
of the minaret so tall.
I hear soft echoes
of the prayer call.

Rectangle is the
mosque's carved wooden door,
filled with a pattern
that reaches the floor.

Octagon is a fountain,
its water so blue.
I wash before prayers
and make my wudu.

Triangle is a **mimbar's** thin set of stairs. We hear a short sermon before Friday prayers.

Arch is the mihrab
that guides our way.
We stand and face it
each time we pray.

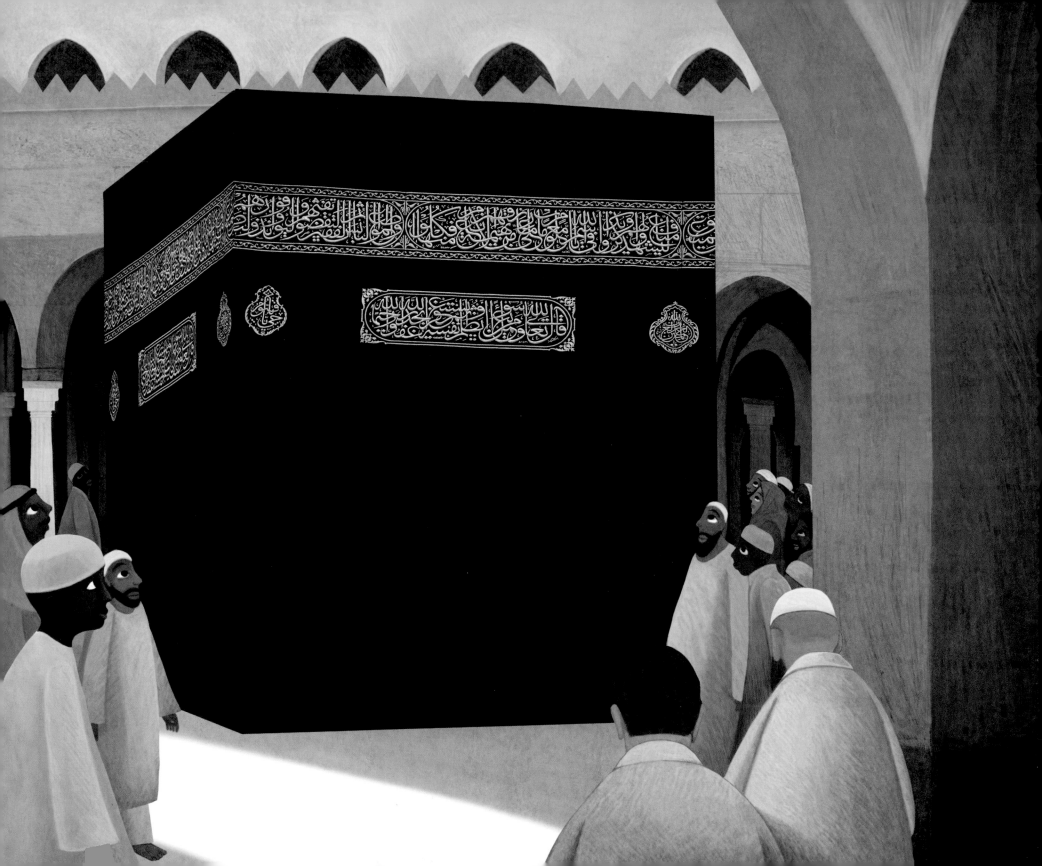

Cube is the Ka'aba,
a most sacred site,
where Muslims worship
each day and night.

Square is a garden
with sweet orange trees,
a hint of jannah
on its fragrant breeze.

Circle is a daff,
a drum large and round.
We fill the air
with its festive sound.

Hexagon is a tile,
bold and bright,
painted with an **ayah**
I love to recite.

Oval is the table
where we break our fast.
When the sun sets,
it's **iftar** time at last.

Diamond is the design
on my new Eid clothes:
A kaftan so long
that it reaches my toes.

Crescent is the moon,
brilliant in the sky.
It whispers salaam
as the day passes by.

So much beauty
in the shapes that I see
adds to my faith
and the world around me.

Glossary

Ayah (EYE-uh): a verse of the holy Quran, the book that guides Muslims, that may be displayed and recited to affirm one's faith or uplift one in a moment of need.

Daff (daff): a large frame drum commonly used in the Near East and Central Asia, especially during weddings and on Eid. It is often played by women.

Eid (eed): an Islamic holiday. There are two Eid holidays. Eid ul-Fitr marks the end of Ramadan, and Eid ul-Adha is a celebration of life focusing on sacrifice and devotion to God.

Iftar (if-TAR): a light meal eaten at sunset upon completing a fast during the holy month of Ramadan.

Imam (ee-MAM): a community member who leads prayer, recites passages from the Quran, and teaches Muslim tradition and heritage, usually in mosques.

Jannah (JUN-na): the Garden of Paradise, or heavenly abode, promised to people who lead lives of faith and good works. Gardens, offering shade and a quiet place for reflection, are often square-shaped and are a feature of many mosques and palaces.

Ka'aba (KAH-bah): a holy temple in the city of Mecca, the word Ka'aba means "cube" in Arabic. All Muslims face in the direction of the Ka'aba while praying and are required to visit it once in their lifetimes, if they are able, to complete a pilgrimage known as hajj.

Kaftan (KAF-tan): a long dress, worn in parts of the Middle East including Morocco and Tunisia, that often includes a wide belt or sash.

Mihrab (mih-RAB): a niche or wall in most mosques that indicates the direction of Mecca and is often beautifully decorated.

Mimbar (mim-bar): a platform, or pulpit, in a mosque where the imam stands to deliver a sermon before prayers.

Minaret (min-ah-RET): a tower at a mosque, from which the Muslim call to prayer (the athaan) is broadcast.

Mosque (mosk): a place where Muslims gather to remember, worship, and celebrate God, as well as hold community events.

Salaam (sa-LAAM): a greeting that means "peace" in Arabic, often used as a hello or goodbye.

Wudu (wood-do): a ritual washing of the hands, arms, face, head, and feet before prayer.

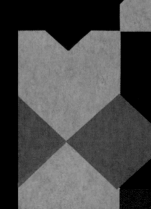